Design/Loris Lesynski, *Laugh Lines Design*

Annick Press Ltd.

We acknowledge the support of the Canada Council for the Arts, the Ontario Arts Council, and the Government of Canada through the Book Publishing Industry Development Program (BPIDP) for our publishing activities.

Cataloging in Publication

Lesynski, Loris
    "I did it because ..." : how a poem happens / by Loris Lesynski ; illustrated by Michael Martchenko.

ISBN-13: 978-1-55451-018-4 (bound)
ISBN-13: 978-1-55451-017-7 (pbk.)
ISBN-10: 1-55451-018-X (bound)
ISBN-10: 1-55451-017-1 (pbk.)

1. Poetry—Authorship—Juvenile literature.
2. Children's poetry.
I. Martchenko, Michael II. Title.

PN1059.A9L47 2006   j808.1   C2006-901211-3

The art in this book was rendered in pencil, watercolor and gouache. Michael says he enjoyed illustrating this book more than his last two visits to the dentist.

The poems themselves were typeset in Utopia, with the titles and labels in an assortment of comic book typefaces such as FaceFront, BiffBaffBoom, Sez You and Spills from www.comicbookfonts.com.

Distributed in Canada by:
Firefly Books
66 Leek Crescent
Richmond Hill, ON
L4B 1H1

Published in the U.S.A. by:
Annick Press (U.S.) Ltd.
Distributed in the U.S.A. by:
Firefly Books (U.S.) Inc.
P.O. Box 1338, Ellicott Station
Buffalo, NY 14205

Printed and bound in China

Most of these poems were originally published in the poetry collections by Loris Lesynski published by Annick Press: *Dirty Dog Boogie, Nothing Beats A Pizza, Cabbagehead* and *Zigzag: Zoems for Zindergarten,* The poems on pages 21, 36, 43 and 48 appear here in print for the first time.

Visit www.annickpress.com

Loris loves getting letters. Send your messages, questions or comments directly to the author any time: **Loris Lesynski, c/o Annick Press, 15 Patricia Avenue, Toronto, Ontario Canada M2M 1H9.** Or you can e-mail her at loris@lorislesynski.com

To the ones who kept us each such good company all the hours we were writing and illustrating this book:

To Molly
—Loris

To Mindy
—Michael

DISCLAIMER

This book is all about rhyming poems but poems DON'T HAVE TO RHYME. If you feel like writing a poem but don't feel like writing in rhyme, GO AHEAD!

Please visit Loris's website at *www.lorislesynski.com* for many more writing ideas.

"I DID IT BECAUSE..."

HOW A POEM HAPPENS

Selected favorites by Loris Lesynski

Illustrated by Michael Martchenko

annick press
Toronto • New York • Vancouver

WHY do you like to write poems?

Where do YOUR IDEAS come from?

What made you write THIS poem?

How do I find MY ideas?

INTRODUCTION:
QUESTIONS THAT KIDS ASK AUTHORS

AUTHOR'S IMAGINATION

Why...?

I did it because —
well the reason was —
it was really because **because...**

I did it because —
because everyone does —
because because because.

I did it I said it
I got it I get it
because because because —

because it was
what it was
BECAUSE...

I really don't know
because.

MAKES YOUR LIPS BUZZ!

CONTENTS

So what's next...?

POEM PREP:

Warming up to recite a poem

Loosen lips.

Flex ears.

Heads up — let the air out!

AIR

Beginners: Practice tongue flapping.
Intermediate: Tongue curls.
Advanced: Tongue twisters.

Hand signal means:
"Join in, everyone."

"Let's get louder."

"Now more quietly."

"Clap to the beat."

Do finger stretches — make your hand gestures and cues very clear.

Warming up to write a poem

Feeling the buh-buh-beat

A good beat *feels* great. Sentences have beats and rhythms right inside them. You can get better at recognizing the beat just by listening for it in songs, poems, jokes and stories. Drum, dance, tap, clap, click, bounce and boogie along.

There are strong beats (DUM) and lighter beats (*da*).

These words are DUM-*da*: skateboard, **pen**cil, **sun**shine, **piz**za, **hun**dred.

These are DUM-*da-da*:   sandwiches   **bas**ketball   **Sat**urday

You can do your name: Jake (DUM)   Jesse (DUM-*da*) A**man**da (*da*-DUM-*da*)   **Nic**holas (DUM-*da-da*)

Can you find a word that fits this rhythm?

da-DUM-*da-da*

rhi**noc**eros

Sometimes a poem idea comes to you when you hear a rhythm you really like, and *then* you find the words to put in.

Here's a rhythm coincidence: the names of the author and the illustrator *both* go **DUM**-da da-**DUM**-da (**Lor**is Le**syn**ski and **Mi**chael Mart**chenk**o).

Dirty Dog Boogie

I **had** a dirty dog
    and I **had** a dirty cat
and I **took** them both to
    the laundromat.

The cat objected
    and the dog complained
so I took them home
    in the pouring rain.

The cat got mad
    but the cat got clean
and the dog was as shiny
    as I'd **e v e r** seen!

So even though they yell
    and even though they yowl
I take them in the rain
    and I take along a towel.

If you have a dirty dog
    and you have a dirty cat
don't take them
    don't take them
        don't take them
        to the
        laundromat.

A Bit of Boogie

A **boogie** is a dance
and a **boogie** is a jive.

A **boogie's** just another way of saying **"I'm alive!"**

Boogie in an elevator.

Boogie in the street.

Anything's a **boogie** if it has a **buh**-buh-beat.

Boogie in a poem.

Boogie when you're blue.

Boogie when you haven't got another thing to do.

Boogie on your bicycle.

Boogie on your bed.

Always keep a **bit** of boogie **go**ing in your **head!**

POE POE POEM

RAH RAH RHYME

YOU can DO one A N Y time!

Top dog, **bottom** dog, **doggie** in between.

Rhyme about a dirty dog?

Rhyme about a clean.

ALL your body listens.
ALL your body hears.

A poem isn't **ONLY** for your doggie little ears.

Feeling kind of crummy?
Run a rhyme instead.

Always keep a **bit** of boogie **GO**ing in your **head!**

Always keep a **bit** of boogie **GO**ing in your head!

Always keep a **bit** of boogie **GO**ing in your head!

11

Dawdle Dawdle

Dawdle dawdle

go so slowly

let the others

rock and rolly

wait a little

ready later

yawning like an

alligator

wrap a shoelace

round a finger

loiter here and there

and linger

dawdle dawdle

t a k e   y o u r   t i m e .

OR

y o u   c o u l d . . .

step on it and *make it snappy!*

hurry make the teacher happy!

do not mosey! do not toddle!

never ever! *do not dawdle!!!!*

Anything's a Drum

anything's a drum drum

    a can can be a drum drum

tabletop's a drum drum

    chair a double chum drum

    drum drum anywhere
    drum drum in the air

knees can be a drum drum

    both of them a fun drum

hands are for a clap drum

    floor is for a tap drum

    drum drum anywhere
    drum drum in the air

elbows touch-each-other drum

    head can be another drum

drumming in the air drum

    drumming anywhere

drum drum anywhere

    drum drum in the air

    drum drum anywhere

    drum

        drum

           drum

Can't Sit Still

No I **can't** sit still

never could

never will

gotta flip

gotta flop

gotta flap until

my bones are bouncing

my shoulders shake

with a jiggle and a wiggle

and I can't make me

STOP.

No I **can't** stand still

never could

never will

gotta jig

gotta jolt

gotta jump until

I've had enough of leaping

and I've had enough of hopping

and I'm thinking now of stopping

and **STOP.**

A Guy's Gotta Move

A guy's gotta move

like he knows where to go

a guy's gotta move

with an ebb and a flow

a guy's gotta know

when to stand

when to glide

a guy's gotta know

inside

Bizzy Boys

Busy boys are bumping thumping

clumping down the halls.

Busy boys are stamping stomping

tromping up the walls.

Yelling boys are making noises—

don't get in the way!

And what are they so busy at?

They're going out to play.

The Bad Mood Blues

You *wake* up in the morning and
you *know* it's there

BAD   M O O O D

BAD   M O O O D

From underneath the covers
you can feel it in the air

BAD   M O O O D

BAD   M O O O D

Everything goes wrong the day
you wake up in the dumps
you know your socks have vanished
and your hair has gone in clumps
your milk is spilling everywhere
your brother has to *poke* you
and everybody's bugging you
and says it's just a *joke,* you
know it isn't fair and know
you're totally upset
and the *day* hasn't even
the *day* hasn't even
the *day* hasn't even

S T A R T E D   Y E T

so whatcha gonna do

when you wake up feeling blue

gotta figure out a way to

get a rhythm to the day

   and   B E A T   B E A T   B E A T

B E A T   B E A T   B E A T

BEAT BEAT BEAT

the BAD MOOD away

BAD   M O O O D

OUT LOUD ALLOWED

Use a story voice when you read out loud. Be dramatic. (Regular voice: "Got any hot dogs?" Story voice: "Once upon a time in the Land of Magic Hot Dogs...")

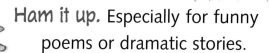

Ham it up. Especially for funny poems or dramatic stories.

Speak realllllly clearly. Try not to mumble. Don't sound flat, shy or bored.

Send your voice out into the world. This is different from shouting. It's called **projecting.**

ECHO-O-O READING

You say a line of the poem, as expressively as you can, then everyone else repeats it after you in the same tone of voice, loudness, expression and rhythm. Sounds fabulous!

The **rhythm** is up to you. Keep the beat going in the back of your mind. *Chugga-chugga-***chuck-***chuck,* maybe. Or *ka-***BONG**, *ka-***BONG**, *ka-***BONG**-*itty bong* **BONG.**

Use hand cues to let the other kids know what to do.

Recite out loud Do it in your own way. Some people are loud and goofy, some are quiet and suspenseful.

Go more slowwwwwly If the words are written well, you can take your time. Use… the…pause…whenever you feel like it.

Practice reciting—you'll get better at out-loud reading fast. While walking to school is a good time to practice a poem. *Not* good times: at the dentist's office, or in the middle of the night.

WOOF

OF

WOOF

WOOF

MEOW?

Sound Effects You can put *woofs*, *meows* and *splats* in poems. *Clicks*, *growls* and *hurrahs* are good too. Also *roars*.

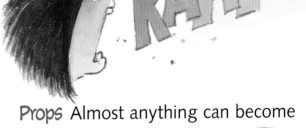

RAAA

Props Almost anything can become a microphone …a hat …or even a dog or cat.

Actions and Gestures are as interesting as words and the beat. Move your legs and arms, fingers, shoulders and feet.

You can even roll your eyes at parts of poems.

Sounds & Wordplay

Some words *sound* like sounds:

purr CRASH click BUZZ THUD

Some words *sound like* what they *mean.*

slippery whisper flicker ring

DANGEROUS! soft

Some words are naturally roly-poly or melodious.

marmalade SATURDAY

absolutely

When you really listen to the sounds of words, it's like tasting new flavors. Play with words. Make up some new ones. Even invent names!

GRISMAL: Loris made up this word for a gray, rainy, dismal day.

PSHOO! PSHOO! The sound a kitten makes when sneezing.

MR. SMUDGELY QUIRKS could be the name of a new principal in a story.

JUMPSTER: a good name for a dog that does a lot of—you guessed it—jumping.

On Zaturdayzzzz

"Zo, zo, whaddya zay?
Whaddya wanna do today?"

I sez to myzelf,
"Myzelf," I zay,
"what'll I do, will I do today?"

I ask my eyez.
I ask my noze.
I ask my feet
and all my toez.
I ask them every Zaturday,
"Whaddya think we should do today?"

Zo many choices, zoon to begin.
But firzt I
alwayz
alwayz
alwayz
end up
zleeping in.

SCHOOL BAKE SALE

21

Mozza Mozza

Mozza

mozza

keeto

keeto

do not land-o

on my feet-o!

Do not sting-o,

make me twitchy.

I go "Ouch!"y,

I go itchy.

Mozza mozza keeto hey!

Mozza mozza keeto **hey!**

MOZZA KEETO,

GO AWAY!!!

Nobody Knows

Nobody knows the troubles I've seen,
and gobody goes the gubbles I've geen.
Pobody poes the pubbles I've peen,
for fobody foes the fubbles I've feen.

When wobody woes the wubbles I've ween,
but bobody boes the bubbles I've been,
then thobody thoes the thubbles I've theen,
'cause kobody koze the kubbles I've keen.

23

If I Had a Brudda

If I had a brudda,

I would call my brudda Brad.

Brad'd be the greatest brudda

anybody had.

Brad'd drive me in his car.

Brad'd teach me pool.

Brad'd beat up any kid

dat boddered me at school?

Brad'd give me money

and he'd praise me to our Dad.

Oh I wisht I had a brudda

(a really poifect brudda)

like imaginary Brad.

Fidgetfidgetfidgeting

(Background chorus: Fidgetfidgetfidgeting, fidgetfidgetfidgeting …)

OH NO!! My toe is fidgeting.
Oh ho! My leg is fidgeting.
And now my knee is fidgeting,
so all of me is fidgeting.

> Fingers twitchy fidgeting
> My face a-fitchy twidgeting
> An antsy dancey fidgeting
> I fidget everywhere.

> But **wait**—my toes stop fidgeting…
> and now my knee's not fidgeting….
> My leg's no longer fidgeting…
> now none of me is fidgeting.

> **Fingers still.** *(No fidgeting.)*
> **Statue face.** *(No fidgeting.)*
> **I take my place.** *(No fidgeting.)*

> **No fidget**
> a n y w h e r e.

No Smirchling Allowed

A brand new teacher came today
    from one of the other schools.
"Be serious," she ordered us,
    "and listen to my rules.

"There won't be any splurching,
    and you're not allowed to flitz.
Anybody caught klumpeting
    will put me in a snitz.

"No floozering at recess.
    Grufflinking's not permitted.
And anyone who splubs outside
    will *not* be readmitted.

"When you put your hand up,
    I don't want to hear a bloud.
And let's be clear that while
    I'm here, no sneeping is allowed."

I was truly baffled, but I didn't
    want to show it.
What if I was flitchering and
    didn't even know it?

We sat as still as statues.
    No one made a peep.
All of us were terrified
    we'd accidentally sneep.

We didn't have a clue about
the rules that she was using.

Can *anyone* be good when being good
is so confusing???

Pick a topic, ANY topic

Need an idea? Try this: start with *any* topic, even one that's kind of ordinary, even boring. Write it down in a bubble. Then, fast as you can, add more bubbles for whatever comes to mind. Then add more connections to the connections. Your ideas will surprise you! **Clustering** like this works for coming up with ideas and also for solving problems.

ordinary idea:
stripes

socks

referee or prison uniforms

what if everything kids wore was striped, would you get dizzy looking at them?

pencils lined up

grill in the front of a limousine

slats in a fence

cake with a lot of layers

pencils lined up

stripes on zebras and snakes, what if people had striped skin?

"earning your stripes" stripes on military officers

poem about funny striped food?

the stripes on bar codes that get scanned at the store, how do they work, could you put these kinds of codes on everything?

racing stripes, can I design a faster racecar?

magnetic stripes on Mars, what do they prove?

Leap and *bounce* in your brainstorming.

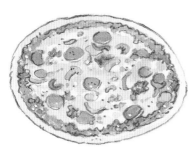

How about **pizza** as a good topic for a poem or two?

Old, Cold Pizza

Old, cold pizza.

    Having breakfast all alone.

Everybody's gone to work.

    There's only me at home.

Wish that someone else was here.

    Pizza, could you say:

"Morning, kid — I hope you have

    a really awesome day."

Pizza Theme & Variations

Porridge too hot?

Porridge too cold?

The story of Goldilocks *could* be told

with pizza.

"Papa Bear's pizza?

Not enough cheese.

Mama's has too many anchovies.

But Baby Bear's pizza?

The best in the wood!"

Said Goldie, "It's almost

un*bear*ably good

pizza."

A dragon can toss a pizza high
    in the air with a flip of its tail,
cook it fast with a blast of flame,
    and eat it with ginger ale.

To fry up a frightful witches' pizza,
    choose between spiders and bugs.
Melt eye of newt and tongue of toad
    and sprinkle it with slugs.

Jack was a pizza delivery boy
    till the day of the Giant's call.
Jack couldn't balance the Party Size
    on a beanstalk quite so tall.

Nothing Beats A Pizza

Nothing beats a pizza
when you're in a pizza mood
because a pizza isn't anything
like any other food

other food is neat and tidy
pizza's *slippy* *pizza's slidey*
(makes me full and satisfied-y
nicest slices now inside me)

When we want to eat a pizza
then it's better having two
'cuz just one pizza's not enough
for me and you
and you and you
and you and you
and YOU.

Nothing beats a poem
when you're in a
poem mood because
you never know
exactly what a poem
might include.
It offers laughs
and often thoughts
and pictures in your head,
and sometimes says,
"Let's look at things this
other way instead."

Make a poem bake a poem
take a poem home
write a pizza poem
in a group or on your own.

Wet Feet
(A Winter Chant)

"How can **any**one be happy

  when they've got **wet feet?**"

This is what I say as I go squishing down the street.

(It always seems to happen when it rains or snows.)

    How can anyone be happy

      when they've got wet feet?

How can **any**one be happy when their feet

  are soaking wet?

I stay away from puddles — but sometimes I forget.

  (My boots are very leaky, that's the reason I suppose.)

    How can anyone be happy

      when they've got wet feet?

How can anyone be happy when their boots are full of sleet?

No one can be happy when they've got wet feet.

(Socks are very soggy when it's slushy in the street.)

HOW CAN ANYONE BE HAPPY WHEN

THEY'VE GOT WET FEET?

Try out
almost
anything
as a topic.
Even...
feet!

Sock Fluff

Down in the corners of most of my toes,

clumping together in bunches and rows,

right out of sight where it seldom shows

      — that's where I keep my sock fluff.

Blue socks make blue fluff and red socks make red.

Striped socks make some of each colour instead.

They stay in at night when I fall into bed

      —red yellow blue bits of sock fluff.

When I'm in the bath and the bits just begin

to start floating away from my soapy wet skin,

    I grab them…

       and dry them…

          and tuck them back in

      —my favorite pieces of sock fluff.

Do ladies have sock fluff in ladylike toes?

    Does everyone *else* have some

      under their clothes?

      Or is it just *me* with this nice little cozy

        collection of personal sock fluff?

...or you could even write poems **about** poems!

A Poem'll Do It

Somebody has to, *somebody* must.

   Somebody's got to say something or bust.

It has to be me, cuz I know what to say.

   I know how I'll do it: a poem's the way!

I'll make it as simple and cool as I can.

   They'll all pay attention and then understand.

A snap to remember and fun to repeat

   here in the classroom or out in the street.

I'll read it aloud on the morning P.A.

   I'll print it on t-shirts

      and give them away.

         In just a few words

            I'll be clear as can be.

               That's how I'll get them to

                  listen to me!

I Hate Poetry!

I *hate* poems.

I *hate* verse.

Nothing makes me feel much worse

than the *ratta-ta-***tat**
of the pounding rhyme
*beat-beat-***beating** on me all the time.

Cat mat hat.
Ink pink clink.
Dump them all in the kitchen sink.

Teacher, teacher, what would you say
if I read out loud at **you** all day?

I **hate** poetry.

    I **hate** rhyme.

That's why I'm ending
    without one.

Go Away, Poem!

Go away, poem—
     it's the middle of the night.
One good clue is there isn't any light.
     Look, I'm in pajamas
          and I haven't got a pen,
and my notebook's in my backpack
          and it's somewhere in the den.

     Go *away,* poem. I'm supposed to be asleep—
          something that's impossible if you decide to keep
               running all around my head,
          dancing on my brain
               sounding more and more excited
     as you make up each refrain.

          Okay, poem—I'll get up and write you down.
               Find a pencil, find some paper
                    (trying not to make a sound).
               But if I'm getting out of bed
                    and turning on the light,
                         you better sound as good
                              tomorrow morning
                                   as tonight.

About me me me me me

Guess what—you really **are** a very interesting person! And guess what else—you're going to change— a little today, then some more tomorrow, and a lot by next year. It's a great idea to write down **information** about yourself right now today, and also your **observations** and **opinions.** It's fun to write about your-self! You can draw pictures to go with the writing, too.

My biggest wish is...

Everything that's in my room at this moment

The superpower I'd most like to have

Something unusual about my friends/my dad/my dog

What I'd do with a million and a half dollars

I wish I knew...
(a particular person? how to do something special?)

My current favorites:
friends, foods, colors, clothes, animals, books, movies, ways to spend Saturday, things to do in the summer, tv shows, games

I wish I could...

I'm fascinating, absolutely fascinating!

I especially like...

My favorite people

25 big things I'll do in my life

The most important life rule, in my opinion

What I can't stand

P.S. Remember to put the **date** on your writing, and to save it.

I Look in the Mirror

I look in the mirror
and what do I see?
Someone that everyone else
calls *me*.
This is my hair. This is my nose.
These are my shoulders,
and these are my clothes.
They see me, they know me,
they call out my name.
They seem to believe that
I'm always the same.
But none of my dreams or
my thoughts can be seen.
You can see what I look like
but not what I mean.
Look at me closely with
all of your eyes—
all you will see is
my perfect disguise.

41

Walking Past Kindergarten

They write their names in sparkle glue.

They fingerpaint in green and blue.

They'll sing a song, they'll have some juice,

they'll brag about whose tooth is loose.

And when the door is open wide,

I just can't help but look inside

and wonder if a part of me

might sometimes wish that I could be

back there again, for just a day—

but no, I hurry

on my way.

"Me, My, Mine!"

"Me!" says the monkey. *"Me! My! Mine!*
It's only me that matters and
I matter all the time."

But *you*, you're sort of helpful
and you're often kind of kind,
and you care and share a little,
and it seems you always find
that everything is better
and we have a better time
every time we get away from
ME! ME! monkey mind.

43

INSPIRATION SPARKS!

Need a spark to start a story, find a poem or just write down some observations? Try one of these.

THE MAGIC T-SHIRT

THE STORY OF AVALANCHE MALONE, THIRD-GRADE TERROR

THE TWELFTH UNICORN

Write your name down backwards. Who would that person be?

THE NOISIEST NOISES I KNOW

WRITING STARTERS

"One at a time," said the monster...

If I had a lot of money...

Skyscrapers...

What matters to me most...

The Nose Thief

Do teachers ever...?

Planet Pizza

The Most
_____
in the World

Write a letter to yourself at 21

THINGS THAT CRUNCH

INVENT YOUR OWN SLANG

Dragon Summer Camp

GHOST GOALIE

"My Funniest Friend"

HOW TO:

- handle bullies
- escape from quicksand
- get over feeling shy
- make a million
- invent a brand new candy or sport or bicycle

How many yellows...?

Complaints Department:

The Worst Time I Ever Had

Things That Are Excruciatingly Boring

What Makes Me Really, Really, Really Mad

A Taste So Bad It Should Be Against the Law

What Most Needs to Change in the World

SURPRISE FRIES

WHY I LOVE BUGS

THE PERFECT ROOM

When you get home from school today and open the door of your room, it will have been magically transformed into the most fabulous place you can imagine.

What's it like?

EXTREMELY SILLY IDEAS:

- ANTI-GRAVITY SCHOOL
- HOW TO BE A PARTY POOPER
- WE HAVE AN INVISIBLE TEACHER!
- HOW DIFFERENT THINGS WOULD MELT
- HOW POTATOES WOULD SOUND IF THEY TALKED

Write a nonsense poem for kids in kindergarten. Use lots of **ZZZ**s.

Can you take a word and play with it like mosquito (mozza mozza keeto keeto) on page 22?

Any other ideas for INSPIRATION SPARKS?

E-mail them to me for my website to inspire other kids:
loris@lorislesynski.com

45

Just looking around

More than a million kids this morning did almost exactly the same things as you—wake up, have some breakfast, go to school. But even so, *your* day is always **unique**—there isn't another one *exactly* like it anywhere. Give it some sharp attention.

Noticing is free. Observation makes life more interesting.

So — what do you see? What do you notice?

Are there any extremely weird buildings on your block?

What if you found a seashell on the street—where would it have come from? What are your friends' quirks? **What makes your granddad laugh?** How many panels in a soccer ball? **What do you think of the shows on TV?**

Which kid (or teacher) do you think might actually be an alien?

Try this for fun:

Look around. Write down **24 things you've *seen* every single day but never really *noticed* before.** For instance, leaf prints on the road...

Leaves

Leaves were here

they left their prints

in greenish grayish brownish tints

like rubber stamps along the road

an autumn message left in code

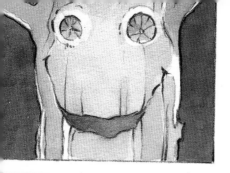

Faces in Places

That cloud in the sky,
    the bark on that tree,
        looking at
        looking at
        looking at
        me.

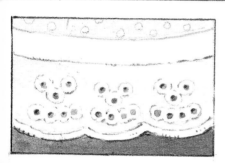

There, where the shapes and
the shadows connect—
faces in places you'd never expect.

Here, see the eyes, and a mouth, and a nose.
Lace-faces howl on the curtain in rows.
Electrical outlets are faces in shock.
A face on a doorknob,
    a mouth as a lock.

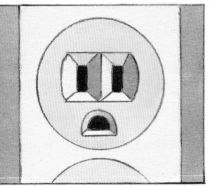

Faces the strangest when
    suddenly seen
in the knobs and the bolts
    of a silent machine.
Faces on flowers and faces on cars.
Sometimes I think there's a face in the stars

Some faces grinning, some faces sad.
Faces found laughing, hysterically glad.
Faces that frown and faces that stare
Once you start looking, they're

                e v e r y w h e r e .

Sunpuddles

Puddles of sun
    fill the living room floor
they spill in the windows
    and slide in the door
shining so hard
    on the tables and chairs
they melt just like butter
    and drip down the stairs.

49

"I wonder...?"

Life is **full** of mystery.

Why are people people and iguanas iguanas?

What does it mean to be alive?

What happens when a person or an iguana

or anything else alive dies?

What is beyond all the stars?

Sometimes you wonder so much about something,

it's exasperating. It almost feels easier to shoo it out of your

mind than to put up with all the not-knowing.

Put your wondering in a poem instead.

Then you can carry it around at the back of

your thoughts for the day you find

some of the answers.

Questions are excellent topics

for writing funny poems,

if that's something

you like to do.

Who Invented Socks?

Every time there's something new,
    ideas are behind it.
Someone took just one of them
    and brilliantly combined it
with just one more or maybe four
    and then experimented,
rearranging all of it till
    something was invented.

All the complicated things that
    came from just a thought!
But what about the simple things
    that matter quite a lot?

Who invented socks?
    Who invented shoes?
Who came up with bicycles?
    and all the different glues?

Who invented macaroni?
    Who invented cheese?
Who invented telephones?
    Who invented keys?

Who invented baseball?
    Who thought up the bat?
What could I invent today
    that's *just* as good as that?

Hello?

Curious

Do rubber bands melt
    if you cook them on high?
Does my blood taste as good
    to mosquitoes as pie?
Do ghosts really happen?
    Are dragons pretend?
If you ate much too much,
    would your bicycle bend?
Does anyone know
    where the universe stops?
Can icicles kill you
    if one of them drops?
If everyone, everywhere
    jumped up at noon,
would the Earth take a swerve
    and end up on the moon?

Mud

What is mud? I do not know.

Where's it come from? Does it grow?

Mud is what it is and so

all it is is

MUD.

A little earth, a little rain,

mixed together. What's its name?

MUD.

The garden when it's very wet,

and has no grass or flowers yet—

MUD.

The bottom of a puddle when

you jump right in and out again—

MUD!

Home Sweet Eyebrow

There are creatures
in my eyebrows.
    They are very, very small.
They live their lives serenely,
    never bother me at all.
I'd never even know
that they were there
    unless I'd seen
a scan enlarged and printed in
    a science magazine.
            They look like worms in armor,
                and they never wander far.
            You can't believe from pictures
                just how small they really are.
            I don't much like to think about
                them living way up there,
            families of tiny mites
                on every eyebrow hair.
                    We have a lot of gadgets
                        in the classroom, but I hope
                        the one we never get is an
                            electron microscope.

What I'd Like to Know

Do teachers ever giggle?

Do teachers ever drool?

Do teachers ever wish
they didn't have to
go to school?

Do teachers ever end up spending
recess all alone?

Do teachers ever miss me when
I'm sick and staying home?

When teachers get together with
their friends at half past three,
do teachers have as good a time
as all my friends and me?

Where IDEAS come from

An ice cream cone can't write a poem.

A snowman can't tell a story.

Animals can't make notes about what's going on around them.

Only **HUMAN BEINGS (like you)** can write poems, stories, songs and jokes. Also opinions, observations, fantasies, histories, adventures, movies and biographies.

Where do the IDEAS for all of this writing come from?
From your own human brain and human eyes and ears. Get very good at looking out for your own ideas. Say "Listen to me!" to yourself a lot. (Don't say it out loud, though, or people will think you're bananas.)

Cabbagehead

I need a brain that's brilliant.
I need a head that hums.
I need a head that's ready when
a good idea comes.
Sometimes I'm a cabbagehead.
Sometimes I'm a star.
Always I'm amazed by where
my best ideas are.

I Need an Idea

I need an idea
need it fast
need a good one
that'll last
need it *here*
need it *now*
need it fizzing
need it *wow!*
need a
full-of-buzz idea
best-there-ever-was
idea
here, idea!
come, idea!
let me hear you hum,
idea

Hi, Ideas! My Ideas!

I got a good idea,
    then I had another three.
Forty-seven more'd make a genius
    out of me.

Good ideas,
    bad ideas,
        some I'm-glad-I-had
            ideas

Come, idea,
    here, idea.
        Whisper in my ear, idea.
    Here, idea.
        Come, idea.
        What will you become,
        idea?

Start one here. Start one there.

Start ideas anywhere.

one idea

    two ideas

        bright ideas

            new ideas

fast ideas

slow ideas

yes! ideas

no! ideas

round ideas

sound ideas

weird ideas

found ideas

sports ideas

art ideas

kind ideas

smart ideas

"**how?**" ideas

"*why?*" ideas

gotta love them,

my ideas!

FINDING RHYMES
in a snap

B...	L...
BL...	M...
BR...	N...
C...	P...
CH...	PL...
CL...	PR...
COM/	PRE...
CR...	PRO...
D...	QU...
DE/	R...
DIS/	RE/
DR...	SH...
EX/	SK...
F...	SP...
FL...	ST...
FR...	T...
G...	TH...
GL...	THR...
GR...	TR...
H...	UN/
IN/	V...
J...	W...
K....	Z...

Use **Loris's Rhyme Chart** to find rhymes fast. Take a word you want to rhyme—for example, **FEET**—and go through the list adding the **EET** sound to each of the endings. You'll get some good rhymes—beat, cheat, complete, repeat, wheat, zeet. *Zeet?!*

ABOUT WRITING

Throughout history, human beings have always enjoyed rhyming.

Rhyme *feels* good. It makes your ears happy, your brain work better. It makes you feel like moving, dancing, marching, singing. Most songs are rhyming poems put to a tune.

You could write a poem for a special occasion or an ordinary one, about something terrible or fabulous that happens, about anything you want, long or short, rhyming or non-rhyming. Spend that extra bit of time to polish and revise your poem. Get it just right. People will love it. They'll remember your poem for a long, *long* time.

Hey, aren't you the guy who wrote that cool poem back in Mrs. Mackay's fifth grade?

IN RHYME

Some rhymes are ordinary:

CAT — HAT

Some are a little surprising:

But it's interesting rhymes that make your poems exciting:

* Listen to how wonderful some words sound together. They make their own rhythms.

Need a way to get started? Use the rhythm of a poem or song you like, and put your own words in place.

6 SPECIAL TIPS FOR WRITING IN RHYME

• **Read** poems and rhyming stories that are really good, such as *Casey at the Bat*, *Jabberwocky*, or any good book of verse for kids. Reading out loud to yourself is excellent.

• **Use pauses.** Remember… that… pauses… are part of the beat.

• **Use a thesaurus.** This is a book full of synonyms. You can also find one on the Net. If you want to find many ways to say someone is *grumpy,* for example, it will give you *upset*, *bugged*, *crabby* and *annoyed* just for starters.

Here's a good one: sourpuss.

• **Repeat lines** in your poem. See *Dirty Dog Boogie* (p. 9) as an example.

• Hear how some words sound **clumsy** together and others **slide** after one another easily.

• **Write down** little bits of ideas that come to you. Write down words you hear that are funny or interesting.

• **Move the words around.** Poems don't have to sound exactly like regular sentences. Put hard-to-rhyme words in other places in the line besides at the end.

* *sewing machine, submarine, fairy queen, seventeen, velveteen rabbit with tambourine*

HOW ILLUSTRATIONS HAPPEN

PROFESSIONAL ILLUSTRATORS usually do several roughs while they're working out the illustration. This is done on cheap paper. Sometimes they need reference material, like a picture of a submarine or someone to model throwing a basketball. When they're ready, they get out the good paper and other art supplies. There are so many ways to make a picture: paint, pencil crayon, pastels, Plasticine, computer, colored paper, ink, watercolors.

THE ERASER is very important. Taking out the lines you *don't* want is just as important as keeping the ones you do want.

This is a **ROUGH SKETCH.** Illustrators often do quite a few of them until they feel they have it just right, especially for the cover art.

If you fold 4 sheets of paper in half, you'll have a 32-page "book" you can use for your words and illustrations. You can staple or sew the center. The cover should be eye-catching and interesting. Then it will make the reader very curious to read the story.

This is the **FINISHED ART,** on the good paper, with the colors often put on in several layers so they are brighter and deeper.

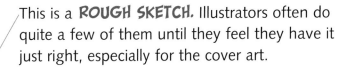

this kind of drawer   not this kind

• Ask someone who draws well to give you short art lessons occasionally.

• Sketch a lot, in pencil. Put the date on your drawings and keep them in a safe place.

• *How-to-draw* books are great and easy to follow, especially the ones about cartooning and perspective. Your library will have books on learning to draw on the **741.5-to-743.8** shelf. Craft stores often have inexpensive drawing books too.

• You'll really enjoy the books about artists listed on page 64.

Some of the rhythmic, refreshing, original poets that you'll enjoy are Lewis Carroll, Shel Silverstein, Karla Kuskin, Dennis Lee, Jack Prelutsky, Sheree Fitch, Brod Bagert, Michael Rosen, Robert Heidbreder, and Robert Service.

There are many, many, many others too.

Go exploring!

GOOD WEBSITES ABOUT WRITING POEMS:

Giggle Poetry www.gigglepoetry.com/poetryclass/cantwrite.htm

Fern's Poetry Club http://pbskids.org/arthur/games/poetry/what.html

Poetry Writing with Jack Prelutsky www.teacher.scholastic.com/writewit/poetry/jack_your_poem.htm

Poetry Writing with Karla Kuskin www.teacher.scholastic.com/writewit/poetry/karla_home.htm

How to Write a Poem: The How-To Manual That Anyone Can Write or Edit http://wiki.ehow.com/Write-A-Poem

Why Teach Poetry? (for teachers, parents, and kids who want to teach themselves)
www.readinga-z.com/poetry/index.html

Poetry Zone
www.poetryzone.ndirect.co.uk/howto.htm

Multicultural Poetry for Children www.mesalibrary.org/kids/reading_elem/poetry.asp

Jabberwocky by Lewis Carroll www.math.luc.edu/~vande/jabberwocky.html

Jabberwocky parodies www76.pair.com/keithlim/jabberwocky/parodies/index.html

ABOUT DRAWING: Learning to draw: www.arts.ufl.edu/art/rt_room/teach/encounters/drawing_encounters.html

About young children using drawing for designing: www.kented.org.uk/ngfl/subjects/dt/halfway/theory.html

Facial expressions: http://images.google.ca/images?q=facial+expressions&hl=en&lr=&sa=N&tab=ii&oi=imagest

ART BOOKS FOR CHILDREN:

www.arts.ufl.edu/art/rt_room/archives/bk_piks.html

www.kidsart.com/store/famous.html

www.powells.com/psection/ChildrensArt.html

www.naturalchild.com/gallery/books.html

www.capitolchoices.org/displaykey.asp?sort=101&key=474

www.powells.com/usedbooks/ChildrensArt.1.html

BOOKS ABOUT ARTISTS, WRITTEN FOR KIDS: There are many more — look in the library.

Linnea in Monet's Garden *about Claude Monet* by Christina Bjork and Lena Anderson

Picasso and the Girl with a Ponytail: *A Story about Pablo Picasso* by Laurence Anholt

Camille and the Sunflowers: *A Story about Vincent Van Gogh* by Laurence Anholt

Four Pictures by Emily Carr by Nicolas Debon

Degas and the Little Dancer: *A Story about Edgar Degas* by Laurence Anholt

My Name Is Georgia: A Portrait *about Georgia O'Keefe* by Jeanette Winter

Diego *about Diego Rivera* by Jonah Winter and Jeanette Winter

A Bird or Two *about Henri Matisse* by Bijou Le Tord

OTHER RHYMING BOOKS BY LORIS LESYNSKI

Dirty Dog Boogie   *Nothing Beats a Pizza*   *Cabbagehead*
Boy Soup   *Catmagic*   *Night School*   *Rocksy*   *Zigzag: Zoems for Zindergarten*

Annick Press, distributed by Firefly Books (see page 2) or go to www.lorislesynski.com

All grownups, please read this book:
Reading Magic: Why Reading Aloud to Our Children Will Change Their Lives Forever by Mem Fox

Parents and tachers, check out **Babies' hands move to the rhythm of language**
http://www.eurekalert.org/pub_releases/2001-09/dc-bh083001.php
Rhythm and the Read-Aloud http://www.bethanyroberts.com/RhythmandtheReadaloud.htm